Cascade Early Learning Center

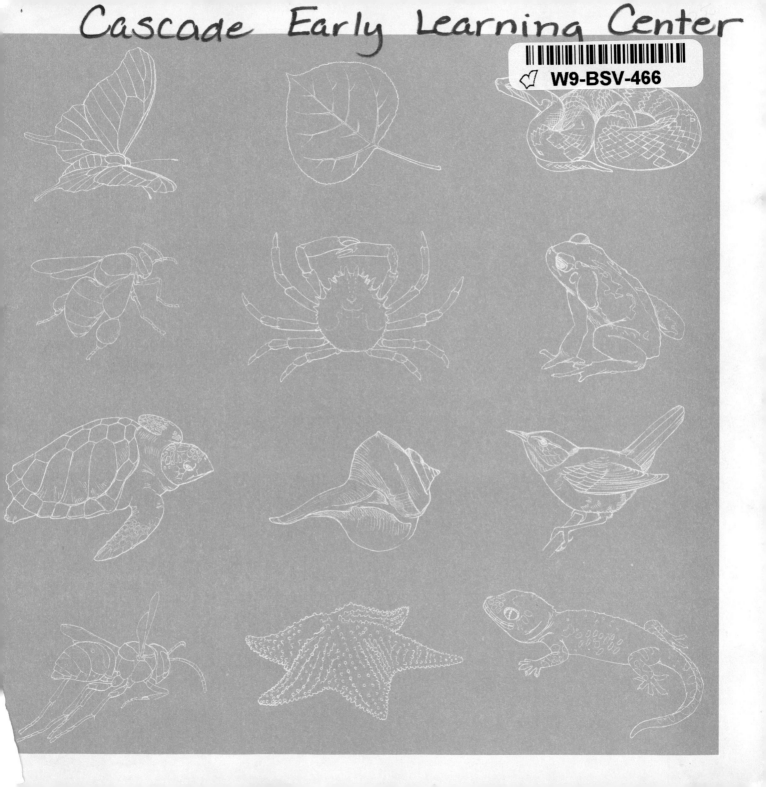

A GOLDEN JUNIOR GUIDE ®

STARFISH, SEASHELLS, and CRABS

By GEORGE S. FICHTER
Illustrated by GEORGE SANDSTROM

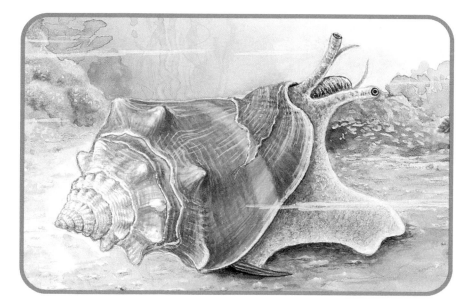

Consultant: R. Tucker Abbott, President, American Malacologists, Florida

A GOLDEN BOOK • NEW YORK
Western Publishing Company, Inc., Racine, Wisconsin 53404

Starfish are *spiny-skinned* animals. In this book, you will meet some of the most commonly seen members of this group. The body of a spiny-skinned animal is covered with many small, sharp spines. Between these are tiny pincers that clamp on to prey or rocks. The mouth of a starfish is on the underside of its body. But don't expect to find a starfish feeding on the beach. Usually, only its stiff, dry skeleton can be found there. A live starfish crawls along the bottom of the sea, using its arms and tiny "tube feet" to grip the ground.

sieve plate

spines

pincers

The Starfish has a flat disk in the center of its body. This disk is called a *sieve plate,* and it has many tiny openings. Water is drawn in through these openings and sent to the starfish's arms.

A Starfish has one red "eye" at the tip of each arm. This "eye" can only sense light and darkness. A starfish usually moves away from bright light.

eye

arm

Did You Know?
About 5,000 different kinds of starfish live in the sea.

The Starfish's arms send water to the many little "tube feet" underneath. As the water is pumped out, each "foot" becomes a tiny suction cup.

"tube foot"

Did You Also Know?
Even though the word *fish* is part of its name, a starfish isn't a fish at all!

3

The Common Starfish

has five arms. It eats clams, other starfish—almost any small, slow-moving sea creature. An oyster bed is a banquet! The starfish wraps itself around an oyster. Then it begins pulling on the shell with its arms. The oyster will hold its shell closed as tightly as it can, but eventually it will tire and open it a tiny bit. The starfish's stomach will then come out through its mouth, and the starfish will squeeze it into the oyster's shell to get at the soft meat inside.

The Common Starfish feeding on an oyster.

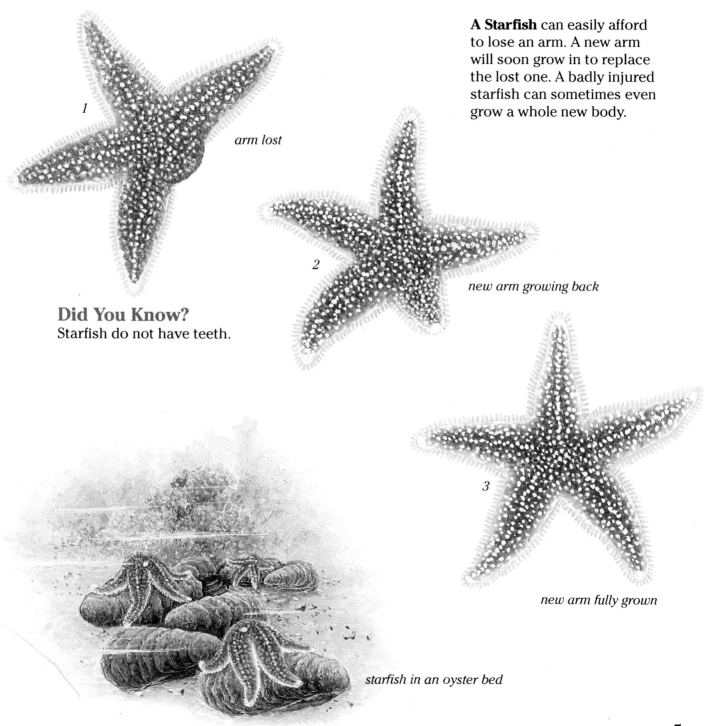

1

arm lost

A Starfish can easily afford to lose an arm. A new arm will soon grow in to replace the lost one. A badly injured starfish can sometimes even grow a whole new body.

Did You Know?
Starfish do not have teeth.

2

new arm growing back

3

new arm fully grown

starfish in an oyster bed

Most Starfish have five arms, but some have six or more. The Sunflower Star starts life with only six arms. It adds more as it grows. Many full-grown Sunflower Stars have twenty-one arms. Some have more than thirty arms!

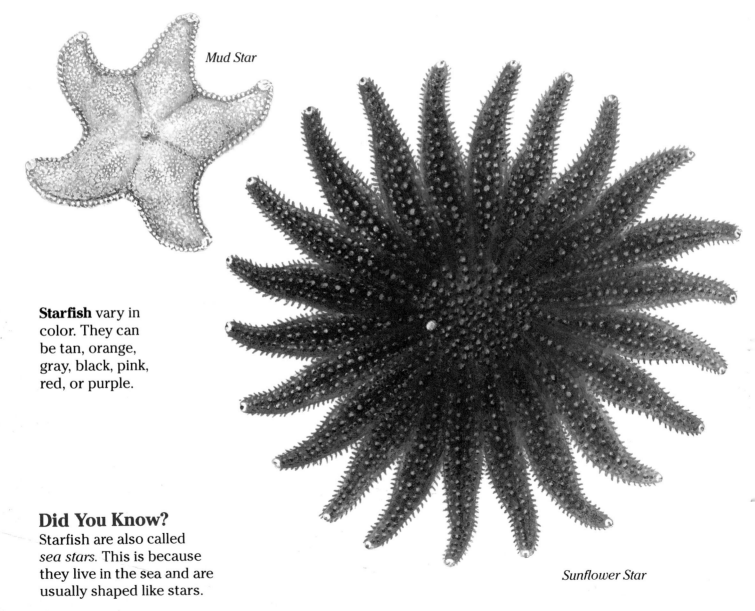

Mud Star

Starfish vary in color. They can be tan, orange, gray, black, pink, red, or purple.

Did You Know?
Starfish are also called *sea stars*. This is because they live in the sea and are usually shaped like stars.

Sunflower Star

6

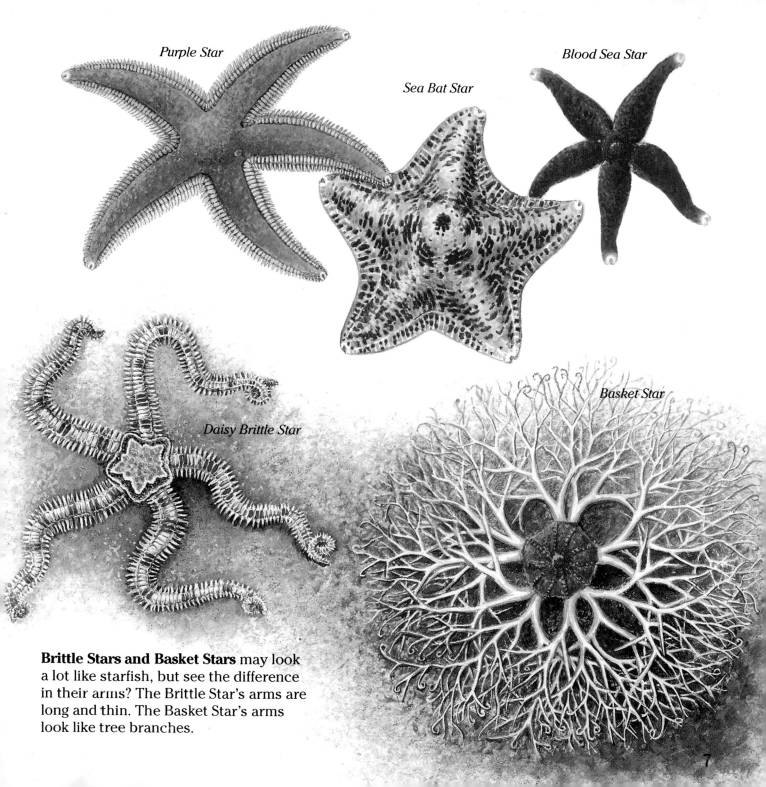

Purple Star

Sea Bat Star

Blood Sea Star

Daisy Brittle Star

Basket Star

Brittle Stars and Basket Stars may look a lot like starfish, but see the difference in their arms? The Brittle Star's arms are long and thin. The Basket Star's arms look like tree branches.

7

Sea Snails live along seashores. They are *mollusks*—sea creatures with soft bodies usually protected by one or more shells. In the next few pages you will meet some of the most commonly seen mollusks and their shells. Snails have only one shell. Sea slugs are snails that have no shell at all. Other mollusks, such as clams and oysters, have two shells.

Snails have an unusual tongue, called a *radula.* The radula has tiny, hard teeth on it. These teeth are used for drilling holes in other mollusk shells, to get to the soft meat inside.

intestine

gill

esophagus

eye

tentacle

mouth

tongue, or radula

mouth

What's Inside a snail?
This "cutaway" shows what
you'd find if you peeked.

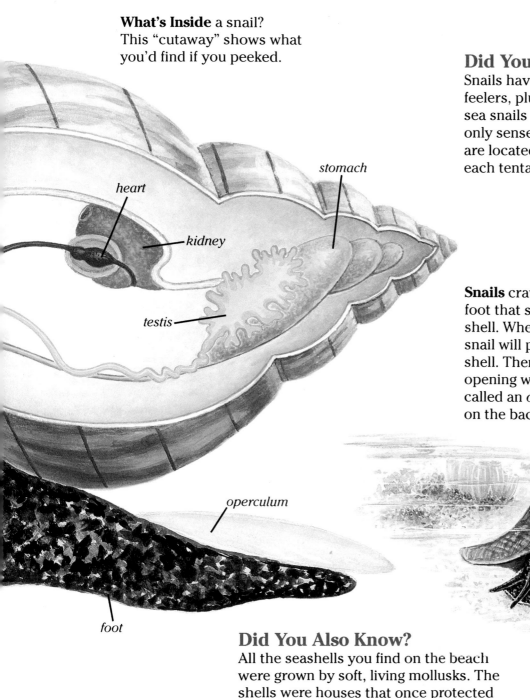

heart

kidney

stomach

testis

operculum

foot

Did You Know?

Snails have two *tentacles,* or
feelers, plus two eyes. In most
sea snails the eyes, which can
only sense light and darkness,
are located near the base of
each tentacle.

Snails crawl along using a
foot that sticks out of their
shell. When threatened, a sea
snail will pull its foot into its
shell. Then it will cover the
opening with a hard shield,
called an *operculum,* that is
on the back of the foot.

Banded Tulip

Did You Also Know?

All the seashells you find on the beach
were grown by soft, living mollusks. The
shells were houses that once protected
the animal from crabs and fish.

9

Moon Shells

Moon Shells are common along beaches on both the Atlantic and Pacific coasts. But even if you do not see a live Moon snail on the beach, you may find signs of one. A Moon snail lays its eggs inside a circle of sand it creates around its shell. The grains of sand are held together with a gluelike substance that the snail produces. This temporary structure is called a *sand collar*. When they first hatch from eggs, Moon snails—and most other sea snails—are called *veligers*. The tiny veligers are carried out to the sea by currents.

shell

Moon Snails feed on clams and other mollusks. They use their huge, strong foot to hold down their prey until they find a way to get inside its shell.

10

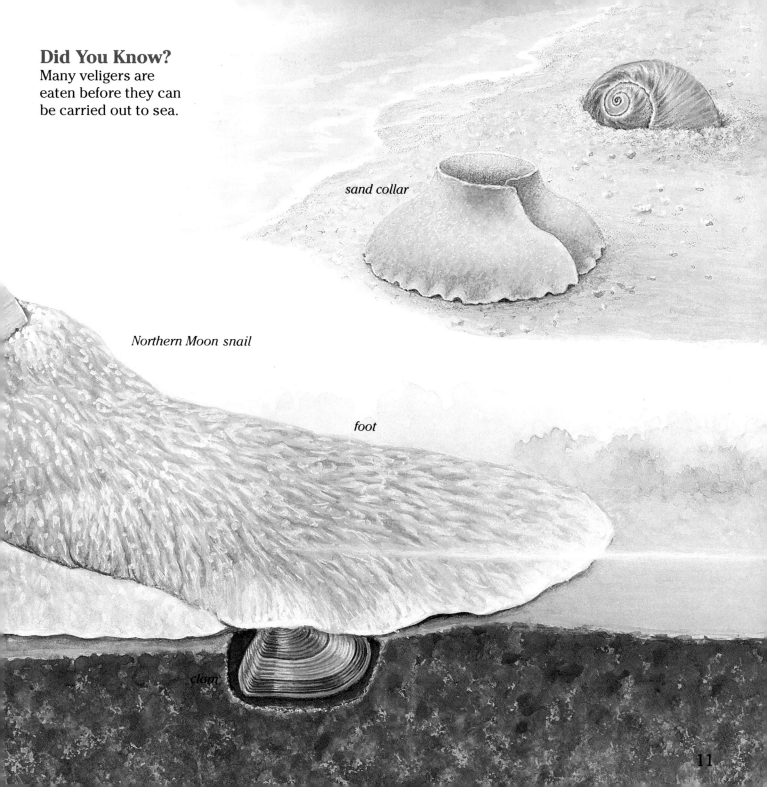

Did You Know?
Many veligers are
eaten before they can
be carried out to sea.

sand collar

Northern Moon snail

foot

clam

11

Periwinkles can be found along most seashores. They are dull-colored and usually quite small. This helps them hide from the birds and crabs that like to eat them. Periwinkle snails use their long tongue to scrape their favorite food, seaweed, from rocks and other hard surfaces. Periwinkles are usually found in shallow water. But some live on tall reeds in marshes or on plants that grow near the shore.

Periwinkles can crawl over rocks. They produce a slippery substance that helps them glide along. But no snail—on land or in the sea—moves very fast.

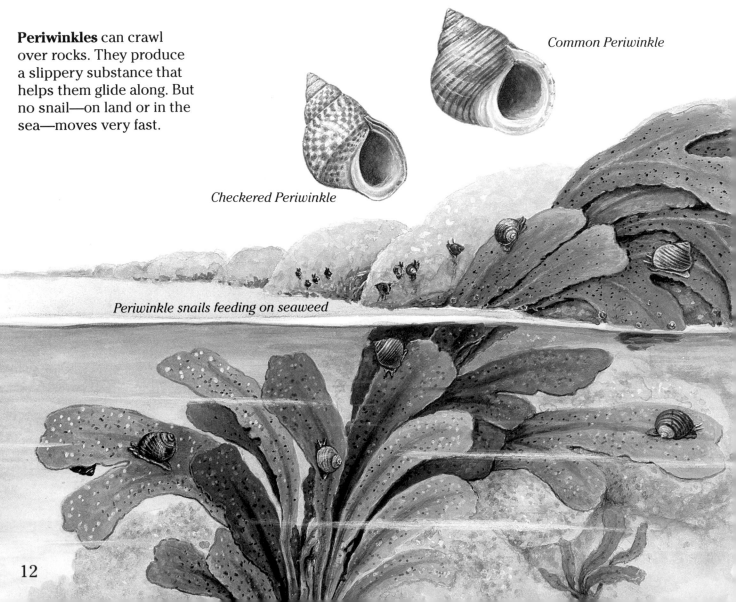

Common Periwinkle

Checkered Periwinkle

Periwinkle snails feeding on seaweed

Did You Know?
It would probably take half an hour for a snail to crawl from the bottom of this page to the top. Even a snail moving as fast as it could would take about five days to travel a mile!

Angulate Periwinkle

Marsh Periwinkle

Ceriths and Horn Shells

are small and slender. They live in groups, or *colonies,* and feed mainly on seaweed. The shells, with many spirals and deep ridges, are usually less than an inch long. You are likely to see lots of these little shells along both the Atlantic and Pacific coasts of the United States.

False Ceriths

Florida Cerith

California Horn Shell

Did You Know?
The eggs of these and
many other snails are laid
in jellylike clumps or strings.

Cowrie Shells

are beautiful, oval-shaped, shiny shells that are often made into necklaces, bracelets, and decorations for homes. In some countries, these shells have been used as money. Cowries are found only in warmer waters. Tiny shells called Coffee Beans are related to Cowries.

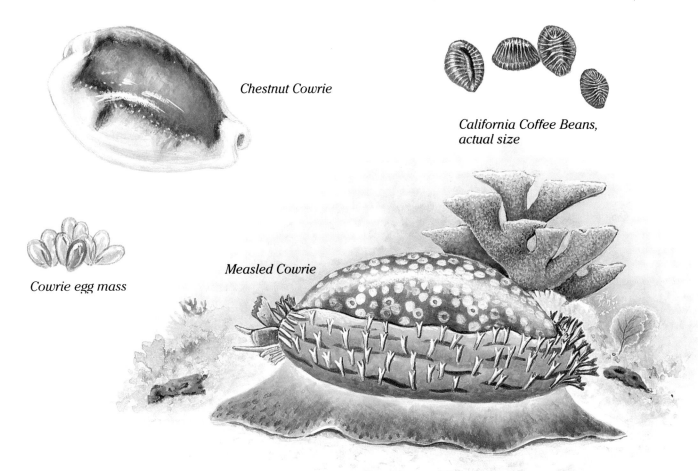

Chestnut Cowrie

California Coffee Beans, actual size

Cowrie egg mass

Measled Cowrie

Did You Know?
A Cowrie snail hides its shell under a blanket of flesh that comes out from its body. This covering keeps the shell polished.

A Female Cowrie Snail
sits on her eggs for several weeks until they hatch.

15

Murex Shells

Murex Shells often wash up on beaches. There are dozens of varieties. Some are small, and some are quite big. Many are thick, heavily ridged, and have long spines, or narrow lines, down the back. Most Murex snails feed on clams, oysters, and other mollusks. They stay in deep water but near the shore.

Apple Murex

Did You Know?
When they feel threatened, Murex snails sometimes produce a yellowish fluid that smells like rotten cabbage! It drives other animals away. After a few minutes in the sun, the yellowish fluid turns purple.

Lace Murex

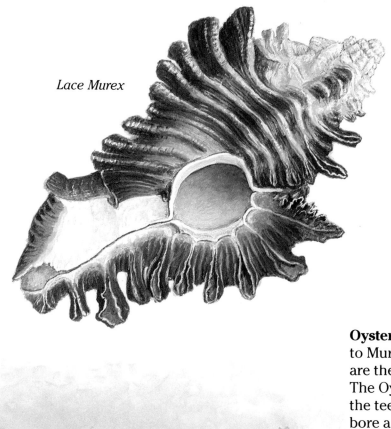

Oyster Drills are related to Murex snails. Oysters are their favorite meal. The Oyster Drill snail uses the teeth on its tongue to bore a hole in the oyster's shell. Then it eats the juicy meat inside.

Oyster Drill

oyster

Cone Shells

are cone-shaped. They have bright yellow and brown markings. Cone snails are found mostly in the Pacific and Indian oceans. Many of them are poisonous! The snail darts out its pointed tongue and stings its prey, mainly sea worms and small fish.

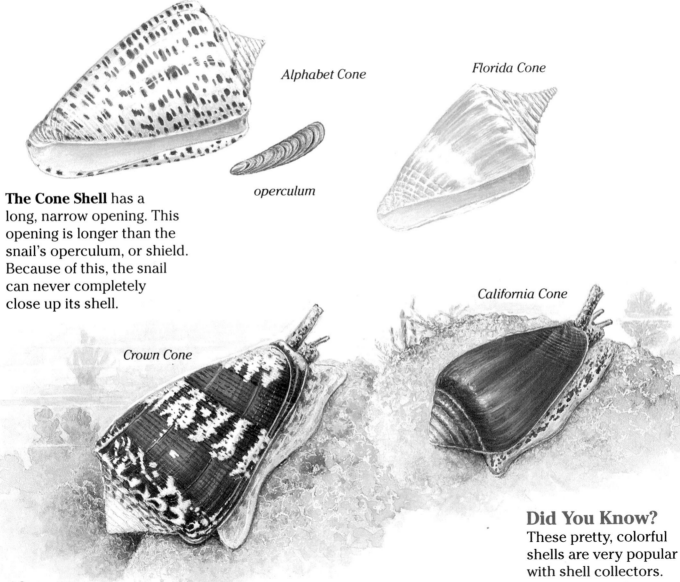

Alphabet Cone

Florida Cone

operculum

The Cone Shell has a long, narrow opening. This opening is longer than the snail's operculum, or shield. Because of this, the snail can never completely close up its shell.

California Cone

Crown Cone

Did You Know?
These pretty, colorful shells are very popular with shell collectors.

18

Whelks

Whelks are among the biggest sea snails found along the shores of the Atlantic Ocean. The largest are the Lightning Whelks. These can measure more than a foot long. Knobbed Whelks are slightly smaller. Whelks feed mainly on clams and other double-shelled mollusks. They use their foot and the edge of their own shell to pry open the shells of their prey.

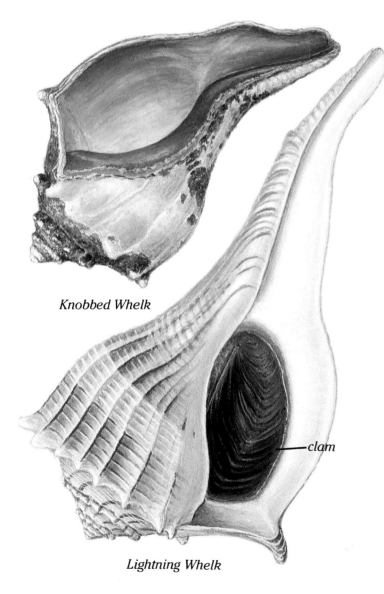

Knobbed Whelk

—*clam*

Lightning Whelk

Whelks lay their eggs in long strings. Sometimes these wash up on beaches after a storm. The egg cases are shaped like saucers. Inside, you might find several perfect little baby shells.

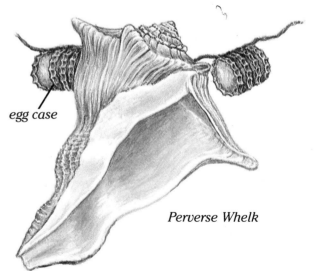

egg case

Perverse Whelk

Did You Know?

Shells can be "left-handed" or "right-handed." Hold the shell with its top end up and the opening toward you. In some shells, you will see that the opening is on the left. In others, it is on the right.

Olive Shells

Olive Shells are popular with collectors. They are usually shiny and are yellow and brown in color. You can find the best ones along the beach just after the tide comes in. The snail itself looks like a fatty glob. You probably would not recognize it as a snail even if you stepped on it. Olive snails have a special storage pouch on the underside of their foot. When they find a juicy meal, they put it in this pouch. Then they dig down into the sand and nibble away on their catch.

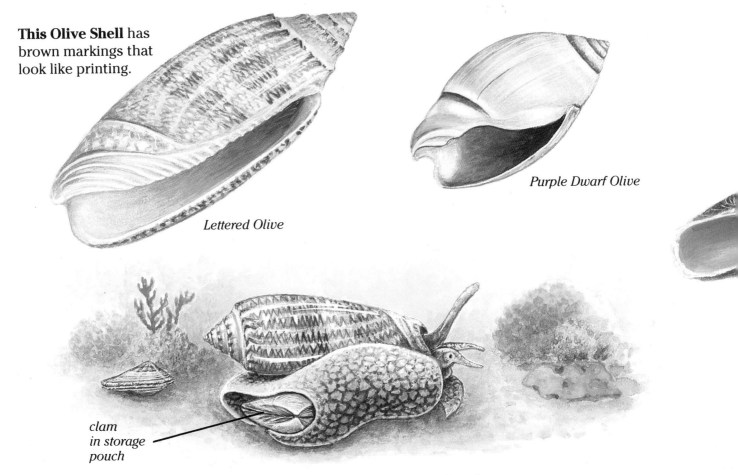

This Olive Shell has brown markings that look like printing.

Lettered Olive

Purple Dwarf Olive

clam in storage pouch

The Olive Snail covers part of its shell with a soft "blanket" formed by its own body.

Tulip Shells

come in many sizes. Small ones are less than 6 inches long. But giant ones found along the Florida coast include the 2-foot-long Florida Horse Conch. Tulip snails live mainly in warm seas. They like to eat other mollusks, especially clams.

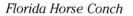

Florida Horse Conch

The Florida Horse Conch is strong. It attacks and kills other large sea snails with its powerful foot. Then it eats them in their shells.

Banded Tulip

Crown Conch

21

Conch Shells

Conch Shells are familiar even to most people who never go to the seashore. These big, beautiful shells are often used for decoration. If you hold the opening of one to your ear, you may think you hear the "roar" of the sea inside. But what you really hear is the sound of air bouncing around the inner chambers of the shell.

Queen Conch shells may grow to be a foot long. Another name for the Queen Conch is *Pink Conch*.

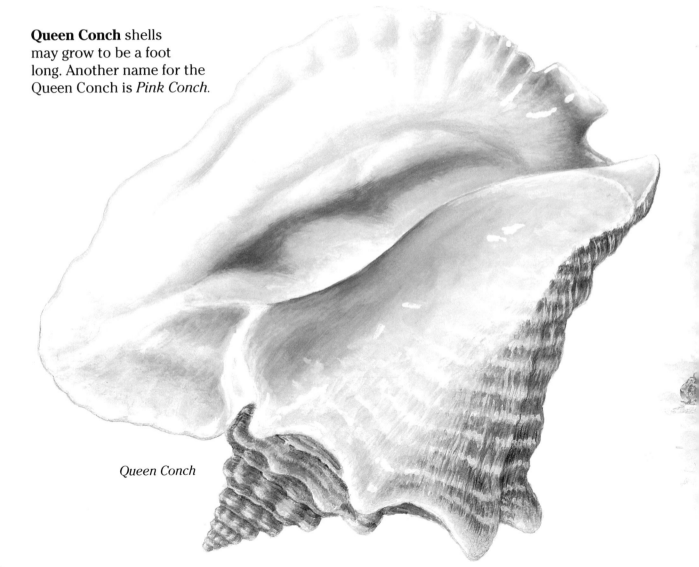

Queen Conch

Conchs have colorful eyes on the ends of short stalks. Attached to the stalks are the tentacles.

eye

tentacle

Conch Snails get about by leaping. They push their foot far out and use its hard, clawlike tip to anchor themselves in the sand. Then they lift up their shell and jerk forward!

Florida Fighting Conch

foot

clawlike tip

Sea Slugs are sea snails that have no shells. They come in unusual shapes and bright colors. Most sea slugs live underwater and are almost never found on beaches. They feed on other animals. Each kind of slug usually has a favorite food. Some slugs like to eat *anemones*—sea creatures that look almost like flowers. The anemones contain tiny "packets" of poison that the sea slug stores in its gills. If a fish tries to eat the sea slug, the "packets" explode and sting the fish.

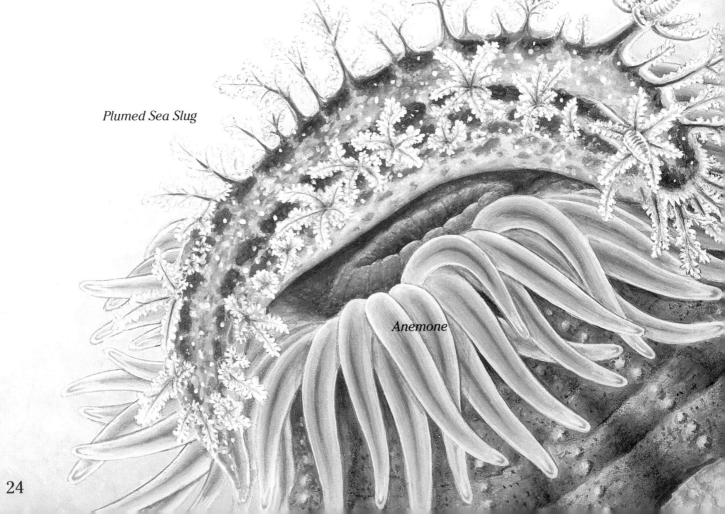

Plumed Sea Slug

Anemone

24

*Bushy-backed
Sea Slug*

A Sea Slug's back contains many protruding structures. These serve as a warning to other animals. They are also part of the slug's digestive system.

Did You Know?
Sea slugs are not the only shell-less shellfish. Some land snails also lack shells.

25

Crabs belong to a large group of animals that have hard outer shells and jointed legs. They live both on land and in water. They have five pairs of legs. These are used for walking and swimming. They are also used for grasping food. If a crab loses a leg, a new one will grow in to replace it. Crabs have two pairs of tentacles, or feelers, and two eyes that are on stalks. They breathe through gills located along the sides of their body. You'll meet some commonly seen crabs in the pages that follow.

Did You Know?
A crab has blue blood!

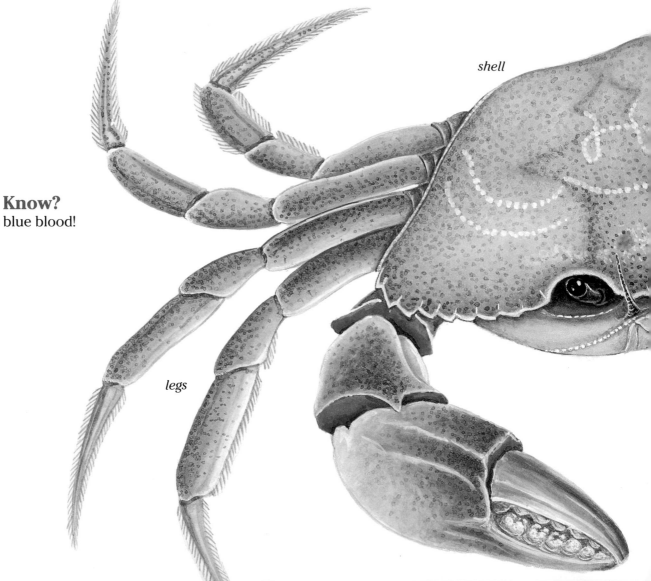

shell

legs

26

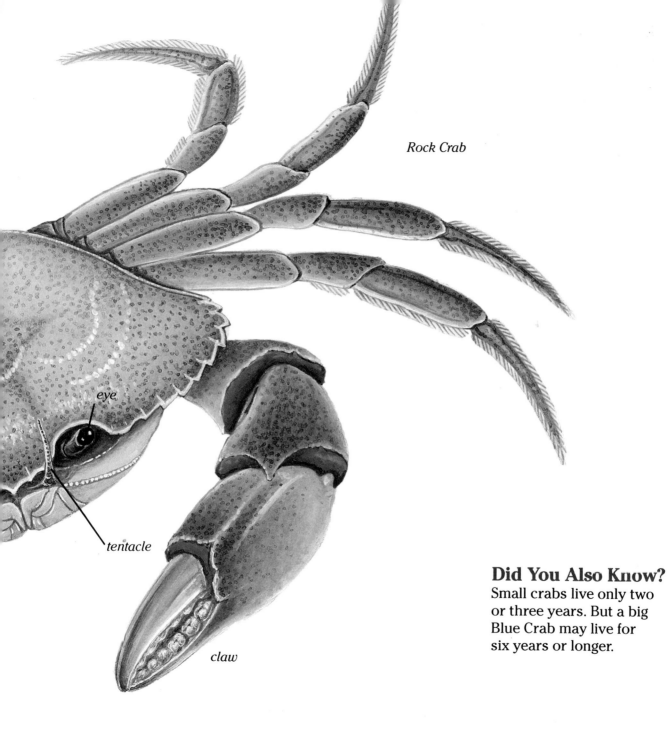

Rock Crab

eye

tentacle

claw

Did You Also Know?
Small crabs live only two
or three years. But a big
Blue Crab may live for
six years or longer.

27

Hermit Crabs

are great at hiding! You see a shell lying on the beach, then suddenly it walks off! If you look closely, you will see that the shell is a Hermit Crab's home. A young Hermit Crab soon outgrows its own shell. It must quickly find a new one. Otherwise, its soft, unprotected parts may be eaten by a fish. The crab can make a home in any kind of shell that is big enough.

A West Indian Top Shell is big and has a large opening. It makes a perfect home for a Hermit Crab!

Hermit Crab inside its shell

The Crab can draw its head and legs into its shell. It will then block the opening with its big claws. The crab's soft body stays firmly anchored inside. A hooklike tail holds the crab in place inside the shell.

Hermit Crab outside its shell

Hermit Crabs are found along muddy and sandy shores. Some are as much as 3 inches long when they are full-grown. Most are smaller. One kind has purple claws.

29

Fiddler Crab

males have one claw, usually the right one, that is much larger than the other claw. The female's claws are equal in size. Males wave their big claw to attract a mate and to warn other males to keep away. The waving claw looks like someone playing a fiddle! Fiddler Crabs like to stay on dry sand, far from the water. They dig deep burrows that may go down 3 feet or more. Fiddler Crabs are fast runners, and they always run sideways! Hundreds travel together in groups called *herds*. Like other crabs, Fiddlers eat the remains of dead animals. They help keep the beach clean.

male Fiddler Crab

If a Male Fiddler Crab loses his large claw, his other claw gets bigger. A new, smaller claw then grows in to replace the lost one.

Did You Know?
Fiddler Crabs are great bluffers. If the male's big claw does not scare off an attacker, the crab will run away!

entrance to burrow

female

Blue Crabs

have paddlelike hind legs that help them to swim very fast. They can swim forward, backward, or sideways! On the beach they always run sideways. Blue Crabs eat dead plants and animals. In the summer they form a kind of natural cleanup crew along beaches and in shallow water. In winter they move to deeper, warmer waters.

male Blue Crab

hind leg

Did You Know?
Crabs can also creep along the bottom of the ocean on their hind legs.

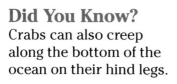

A Soft-shell Crab is a Blue Crab that has recently shed its outer shell. The crab also sheds the lining of its stomach. It cannot eat until the new shell hardens and a new stomach lining is formed. This takes about two days. During this time the crab stays in hiding.

Blue Crab shedding its shell

A Female Blue Crab may produce as many as 4 million eggs a year! These stick to her underside. The eggs later hatch into tiny babies that swim to the surface to feed.

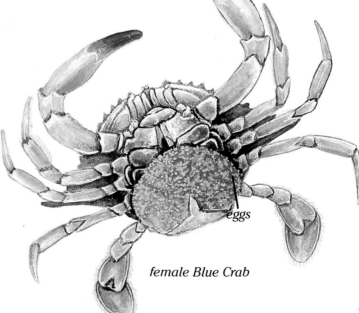

eggs

female Blue Crab

33

Mole Crabs

are common along beaches. They are also called *Sandbugs*. Mole Crabs are very tiny and have a curved plate over their back. They always move backward. As they dig for food, they spread out their long, feathery antennae. The tiny eggs of the Mole Crab are orange. A Mole Crab collecting food leaves a V-shaped pattern in the sand. This pattern is easy to spot, as long as you know what to look for.

V-shaped pattern in sand

Mole Crab

Mole Crabs, with their short, stout legs, can dig rapidly in the sand. They often bury themselves near the water's edge.

Sand Hoppers

got their name because they move about by hopping or jumping. They are also called *Sand Fleas*. Like fleas, their body is flattened on the sides. Although they are related to crabs, Sand Hoppers are not true crabs. Look at how many legs they have!

California Sand Hopper

Sand Hoppers are most often found under seaweed that has been washed up on the beach.

For Further Reading

With this book, you've only just begun to explore some exciting new worlds. To continue, you might look through *Seashores* and *Seashells of the World* (both *Golden Guides*), which contain many details about the species in this book and others. Another Golden Book you might enjoy is *Seashells (Golden Science Close-Up Series)*. Finally, your local library should have a variety of titles on the subject.